HARRY'S MAD

HARRY'S MAD

DICK KING-SMITH

Pictures by Jill Bennett

Crown Publishers, Inc.
New York

Published in the United States in 1987 by Crown Publishers, Inc.
225 Park Avenue South, New York, New York 10003

First published in Great Britain by Victor Gollancz Ltd., 19
Henrietta Street, London WC2E 8QJ.

CROWN is a trademark of Crown Publishers, Inc.
Manufactured in the United States of America

Library of Congress Cataloging-in-Publication Data
King-Smith, Dick, Harry's Mad. Summary: Harry's legacy from
his great-uncle, a talking parrot, proves to be a much more exciting
gift than he ever imagined. [1. Inheritance and succession—Fiction
2. Parrots—Fiction] I. Bennett, Jill, ill. II. Title
PZ7.K5893Har 1986   [Fic]   86-6177

ISBN 0-517-56254-5

10 9 8 7 6 5 4 3

CHAPTER 1

Most people walk down stairs, putting one foot more or less carefully in front of the other, and perhaps holding on to the banisters. Not Harry Holdsworth, oh no, not he!

Long hours of practice had made Harry expert in unusual methods of getting from the upper to the ground floor of the Holdsworths' house.

Some were comparatively simple—sliding down the banister, for example, or rolling down the stairs, or hopping down them, feet together, one step at a time. Hopping down but missing out every other step was a good deal more difficult, and could be made harder still by doing it with hands in pockets, or even—the real test—with hands in pockets and eyes shut.

Harry only attempted this last combination when something told him it was going to be a very special sort of day. On this particular morning, something told him.

As an Olympic athlete, a jumper perhaps, stands poised, breathing deeply, swaying gently back and forth, tensing himself for that indefinable moment when he knows that he is exactly ready to make the attempt, Harry stood at the head of the stairs. His feet were neatly together on the edge of the top step, his hands rammed deep into his pants pockets, his eyes wide, as though to photograph in his mind the other thirteen steps stretching away below him. Seven jumps to make. Harry shut his eyes.

He was about halfway down the staircase when suddenly it all happened. Below him he heard his mother's voice calling "Breakfast!" as she came from the kitchen with a loaded tray; behind him he heard his father say "Watch out, Harry, I'm late already," and right in the middle of Jump Number 5, the mailman rang the doorbell, the dog barked madly (as it always did when the doorbell rang), and the cat dashed upstairs (as it always did when the dog barked madly) just in time to receive Jump Number 6 on the end of its tail. Jump Number 7 took Harry straight into the breakfast tray.

As the yells of the departing cat and the crash and tinkle of breaking china died away, there reigned for a moment a horrible silence, interrupted only by the slurping of the dog licking up raspberry jam.

The breath knocked out of him, Harry lay flat upon the hall floor, as his parents gazed resignedly down at him. Then, through the mail slot in the front door, there sailed a large envelope, which settled, like a bird

3

landing, on Harry's chest. It was a heavy, official-looking envelope, bearing a number of stamps. The stamps were American ones. It was addressed to MR. HARRY HOLDSWORTH.

"It's from America," said Harry, when at last they were all sitting down to a hastily eaten breakfast. "I don't know anybody in America."

"Must be from Uncle George," said Mr. Holdsworth, with his mouth full.

"Who's he?"

"My father's eldest brother; went out there as a young man, finished up as a university professor, must be ninety-something by now, you'll have to tell me about it this evening, Harry, I'm going to be late, I must go," and he drained his coffee and went.

Harry slit open the envelope with a buttery knife. He took out some sheets of paper. On the top sheet was written WILL. HOLDSWORTH.

"Funny," said Harry. "I thought Dad said his name was George."

"It is," said his mother. "Can I see?" She held out her hand for the papers. "It was," she said. "This is a copy of his Last Will and Testament."

She skimmed hastily through a covering letter from a firm of New York attorneys, then glanced at her watch.

"There's a clause in it somewhere that refers to you, but honestly, we haven't got time to look at it now, you must get off to school. We'll go through it when Dad comes back this evening and see what it's all about. I expect he's left you some little keepsake."

All through that day at school, Harry's imagination, always fertile, ran riot. "Some little keepsake" indeed! The fact of the matter is, he told himself, that I have been left something in the will of my very old, very important American great-uncle. Well, to begin with, all Americans are rich, everyone knows that, and as he lived to ninety-something, he would have had all that time to build up a huge store of wealth, thousands and thousands of pounds—dollars, I mean—in fact he'd probably be a millionaire, a multimillionaire, I should think; probably got three or four big houses, all with swimming pools, and a ranch, and his own speedboat, and his own private jet—perhaps he's left me that, I bet I could learn to fly one.

He stretched both arms out wide and began to make warming-up jet noises deep in his throat. Waiting for a voice from the control tower to give him clearance for takeoff, he was quite surprised to hear instead his name called sharply.

"Harry!" said his teacher, "just what exactly do you think you're doing?"

"I was . . . um . . . I was just stretching."

"Stretch your mind for a change, you dreamy boy. I want all those sums finished by recess."

Around him, the other children in the class giggled.

"Harry's mad," someone said.

"Sums!" said Harry to himself as he bent low over the desk, grasping with expert hands the imaginary wheel of Great-Uncle George's (now his) speedboat as it roared across the finish line in a cloud of spray to the cheers of the watching crowds. "The only sums I'm going to need to bother about is adding up all the money he's left me."

By the end of the school day Harry had convinced himself that this fabulously rich great-uncle had by some quirk of fate left him everything that he possessed. Harry was not by nature a particularly greedy boy, but he was an imaginative one, and by now he had gone beyond the three great houses and the speedboat and the executive jet. In addition, he thought he might well receive the largest custom-built Cadillac ever made, and a couple of Rolls-Royces (for occasional use). And, of course, the wealth wouldn't consist only of boring old dollar bills. There would probably be an actual treasure chest, overflowing with diamonds and rubies and emeralds and showers of gold and silver coins.

He stopped outside the candy store on his way home, and looked in the window. I'll be able to buy every single thing in there and never notice the cost, he thought. He put his hand in his pocket. There were two pennies and a two-pence piece in it. "Well, anyway, tomorrow I'll be able to," he said.

Once home, he looked again at his letter from America, but the language of the will was so full of "whereases" and "heretofores" and "hereuntos" and "aforesaids" that he decided to leave it till his father came back from work.

He filled in the time by adding to Great-Uncle George's stable a 1000-cc. Harley-Davidson bike (well, an old model—that he rode when he was younger) and making a noisy circuit of the house.

"Harry," his mother said as he roared along the passage between kitchen and living room, "could you do that up in your room, please?" She spoke with the infinite patience acquired from ten years' experience of being Harry's mother.

"*Vroom, vroom!!*" shouted Harry as he twisted the throttle wide open and set the Harley-Davidson at the stairs. Don't worry, Mum, he thought, I'll soon buy you a bigger house. And Dad can have one of the Rolls-Royces.

When at last he heard the sound of his father's five-year-old Ford, he came downstairs the fastest way (banisters) in a fever of excitement.

"Dad! Great-Uncle George is dead! What d'you think, that letter, it was a will! I can't understand what it's about, can you read it for me? Come on, Mum, Dad's going to read it!"

Mr. Holdsworth sat down at the table and spread out the papers. For a while he read in silence, and then he began to chuckle.

"'What is it?" asked Mrs. Holdsworth. "Has he left Harry something?"

"Yes, he has."

"His fortune?" cried Harry.

"His fortune?" said his father. "No such luck, Harry. The old boy didn't have a lot of money, and what he did have he's left to his university library. No, he's left you what appears to have been his most cherished possession."

"What's that?" said Harry.

"His parrot."

CHAPTER 2

"To my Great-Nephew Harry Holdsworth, whom I have never had the pleasure of meeting, I hereby bequeath my faithful companion of these past forty years, the African Gray Parrot answering to the name of Madison.

"I make this bequest to the aforesaid Harry Holdsworth because he chances to be my only known male relative of an age that I consider suitable, bearing in mind that Madison (a) may live to twice his present span, and (b) like me, has not been used to females."

So ran the early part of Clause 15 of the otherwise conventional Last Will and Testament in witness whereof Professor George Holdsworth had thereunto set his hand.

It went on to detail the provisions that Great-Uncle George had made to ensure that Harry should not be out of pocket by reason of his legacy. "The air fare's paid," said Mr. Holdsworth, "and there's a sum of money to cover the purchase of a large parrot cage and the cost of the creature's food for a year by Uncle George's reckoning. After that time, you're on your own."

"For another forty years?" said Harry in a voice of horror. "You mean I've *got* to keep this bird, and it might live till I'm fifty?"

"Perhaps it'll die before then, darling," said his mother soothingly.

"You never know," said his father. "You may actually like the thing. Perhaps it'll talk. Uncle George was a pretty brilliant man in his day, I believe. Linguistics—that was his line."

"What's linguistics?" said Harry.

"The study of language. All about words, in fact— the parrot's sure to have picked up a few."

"Perhaps I could take it to school," Harry said, brightening up, "on my shoulder. Like that man in *Treasure Island*."

He began to stump around the room keeping one leg stiff, mouthing "Ar! Jim lad! Ar!" and leering dreadfully.

"You're not taking it anywhere," said his mother. "This weekend you and Dad can go and buy a proper parrot cage. I'm not having the thing make a filthy mess all over the house."

"It might be housebroken," said Harry hopefully.

"Don't be silly, Harry. Birds can't . . ."

"Can't what?"

"Well, birds have to . . ."

"They have to do it when they feel like it, your mother means," said Mr. Holdsworth. "Anyway, let's wait and see what . . . what's he called?" he looked again at the will, ". . . Madison, that's right, let's wait and see what Madison's like. He should arrive soon."

And a couple of weeks later, on a Saturday, he did.

News had come from New York of the parrot's time of arrival at London's Heathrow Airport, and now the Holdsworth family waited, with mixed emotions. The whole business, both parents felt, was a great nuisance. Why on earth couldn't old Uncle George have left the bird to a zoo or something? It wouldn't be so bad, they said to each other, if Harry was wildly excited about it, or even moderately happy. As it was, he just looked gloomy. And gloomy Harry was, as he waited for that ring on the doorbell that would herald the delivery van, bringing his companion of the next forty years.

Buying the cage had been fun. There was plenty of money allowed for it, Dad said, so they'd bought a huge one, like a miniature aviary, that hung on a spring from a tall stand. But the more Harry looked at it that morning, its feeders filled with seed and water, its floor sanded, its door open in readiness, the more he worried.

I bet it bites me, he thought. And it'll probably smell. And I don't suppose it'll say a word, just screech all day long or say stupid stuff like "Hello" and "Pretty Polly." And just keep on saying it—till I'm an old man! It isn't even as though I liked birds, and I'm certainly not going to like this one.

The doorbell rang.

Peering into the travel box, standing now on a table in the living room, they could see through the ventilation screen a shadowy shape. No sound came from within except for a scrape of claws on the floor of the box.

"He's alive," said Harry, sounding disappointed.

"Let's get the poor old thing out of it," said his father. "He's had a long trip. Open the lid, Harry."

"He might fly away."

"Shouldn't think so. After all, he's just flown three thousand miles. Must be tired. Go on, open it up."

Doubtfully, Harry undid the catch and raised the lid. He pulled his hand away sharply, as though the travel box contained not a parrot but a poisonous snake.

For a minute or so nothing happened. Then out of

14

the box, silently and slowly, there rose a round gray head with a sharp, hooked beak. On either side of the head was a bright, considering, straw-colored eye.

One of these eyes studied Harry carefully, noting his smallish, rather skinny frame, his mop of bright red hair, his jug-handle ears. Then, levering itself up by gripping the rim of the box with its bill, the parrot climbed out and walked across the table toward him with a rolling sailor's gait. Harry backed away.

"It seems to know you," his mother said.

"Don't be frightened," his father said. "It won't hurt you."

"How do you know?" said Harry.

"Put your hand out. See if it'll walk up your arm."

"You put your hand out," said Harry.

"No, it's your parrot."

"Speak to it," said his mother. "Say its name."

Harry looked at the bird, which had now stopped at the edge of the table and was standing, looking up at him, its head cocked to one side. All he could think of was what a large, sharp beak it had and what cruel, curved talons on its scaly feet. He shut his eyes tight, and put his hand on the tabletop.

"Hello, Madison," he gulped nervously.

Very gently, the parrot stepped onto Harry's arm.

Very gently, it climbed slowly up and perched on his
shoulder. Very gently, it nibbled at the lobe of his ear.

Harry opened his eyes and a grin of relief spread
over his face.

"He likes you," his mother said.

"He's nice," his father said.

"Hello, Madison," said Harry again, this time in a
much more confident voice.

The parrot said nothing.

"Perhaps he'll talk once he's had something to eat," said Mr. Holdsworth. "Stick him in the cage, Harry. He must be hungry."

And indeed, as soon as Harry moved to the parrot cage and stood beside its open door, the bird stepped off his shoulder and waddled inside. It drank thirstily and then settled down to eat, cracking up sunflower seeds in that powerful beak, and watching them all with one or the other pale, intelligent-looking eye.

But despite all their efforts to encourage it during the remainder of that first day, it uttered no sound.

"Pity," said Mr. Holdsworth that evening. "You'd have thought Uncle George would have taught it to say something in all those years he had it."

"I suppose it's just one of those that doesn't," said Harry's mother.

"Must be. Just a dumb animal. Well, time you were in bed, Harry. Good night, old chap."

"Good night, darling," his mother said.

He was halfway up the stairs when he thought he heard a voice calling, "G'night, Harry."

"Good night, Dad," he called back, and then it struck him that the voice was somehow different from his father's, more nasal, more twangy.

He went back down and into the living room, but his parents had left and it was empty. Only the parrot sat motionless on its perch. "Madison?" said Harry. "Did you say something?"

CHAPTER 3

I suppose it must have been Dad's voice, was Harry's last thought before he drifted into a dream-filled sleep where parrots gabbled at him in a language he could not understand and he could not reply.

The dreams turned at last into a nightmare in which he became very tiny—the size of a sunflower seed—and he knew that at any moment a parrot would pick him up in its great hooked bill and crack him open.

Harry woke with a start. He looked at the luminous face of his watch. It was five thirty. Outside, the day was thinking of getting light.

He lay still for a minute, enjoying the relief of his escape from the nightmare parrots and thinking about the real one downstairs. Okay, Great-Uncle George doesn't seem to have taught Madison anything, but there's no reason why I shouldn't. They're only mimics after all, not intelligent creatures, just good at copying. All you have to do is keep on saying the same thing over and over again, and sooner or later they catch on. About a hundred times should be enough, I should think. And then, when they've got it, you teach them something else. I'll start now. It's Sunday and Mum and Dad won't be getting up for ages; it's a good time. What shall I start with? I know, I'll teach him to say his name. But then it's no good just getting him to say "Madison." That'd be like me saying "Harry" to people. No, I know, I'll train him to say "My name is Madison."

Harry jumped out of bed, put on his bathrobe, opened the door, and (for once) went down the stairs very slowly and quietly. Closing the living room door behind him, he went over to the parrot cage and stood beside it. It was on a level with his head.

Harry put on his sneering Gestapo-interrogator face. "Ve haf vays of making you talk!" he said between clenched teeth.

The parrot said nothing.

Harry took a deep breath. A hundred times, he said to himself, I'll say it a hundred times. He leaned forward till his lips were almost against the wire bars of the cage, as close as possible to where he thought the bird's ear must be, and, speaking slowly and clearly, as you would to a foreigner or to someone rather deaf, he said, *"My . . . name . . . is . . . Madison."*

The parrot scratched the side of his bare, scaly face with one foot.

"If you say so, buddy," he said clearly, "but that would be a remarkable coincidence. Seeing that my name is Madison also."

Harry's mouth fell open. He felt amazement, embarrassment, wild excitement—all at the same time.

"What's the matter?" said Madison pleasantly. "Cat got your tongue?"

"You can talk?" said Harry at last in a kind of hoarse whisper.

"Uh-huh."

"Properly!"

"Sure. Mebbe a mite differently from you, seeing I was raised in America, but boy, I sure can talk."

"But . . . I thought parrots could only say a few words."

"Depends how well they've been taught. I've spent all my life with a professor of linguistics. Dead now, but what a guy!"

"Great-Uncle George!"

"George Holdsworth was your great-uncle? You're a Holdsworth?"

"Yes. He left you to me. In his will."

Madison scratched the other side of his face.

"Gee!" he said. "That explains it all. They shoved me in that box, drove me to the airport, and next thing I know, I'm at Heathrow. Madison Holdsworth, I said to myself, it's London Zoo for you, I guess. Instead of which I'm back with the family. Boy, am I glad to be here!"

He cocked an eye at the ceiling.

"Thanks, George," he said.

"Why did Great-Uncle George call you 'Madison'? " Harry asked.

"James Madison, fourth President of the United States of America, from 1809 to 1817. Came after Thomas Jefferson and before James Monroe."

"Oh," said Harry. "Why did he call you after the fourth president?"

"Simple," said Madison. "I was his fourth parrot. Washington died in his sleep, Adams got pneumonia, and Jefferson tangled with the cat."

Harry opened the cage door and the parrot climbed out and up onto his shoulder.

"So it *was* you last night," Harry said. "Saying good night to me, I mean."

"Yeah. Kinda slipped out. And then I thought, sleep on it, we'll see what the morning brings. But just now when you came out with that 'My . . . name . . . is . . . Madison' bit, I simply couldn't keep my big beak shut."

"How did you know my name was Harry?"

"Because I heard your mommy and daddy call you that."

"Oh, silly of me—sorry, I haven't got used to the idea that you can understand everything that's said. What else can you do, Madison?"

"I can read, Harry. And, let's see, I can play the piano a bit. 'Camptown Races,' 'Swanee River,' that kind of thing."

"With your feet?"

"With my beak. Oh, and I can use the telephone. One thing I can't do is write. Never been able to hold a pen or pencil properly."

"Gosh!" said Harry. "Wait till I tell them at school!"

He felt the parrot's claws tighten a little on his shoulder, and then Madison said, "Listen, Harry. Something tells me we're going to get along real fine. But I guess there's a little matter we gotta get straight right now.

This business of me being . . . different from the average parrot."

"Yes?"

"Keep it to yourself, Harry. George did, all those years, never told a living soul. He reckoned if it ever got out, we'd have every newspaper man and television interviewer in the States down on us, not to mention scientists wanting to test me or showmen trying to steal me. We just kept it to ourselves. Waddaya say you and I do the same?"

"Ye-es," said Harry. He sounded doubtful.

"You sound doubtful," Madison said.

"Well, it's just that . . . it was just the two of you, wasn't it, you and Great-Uncle George?"

"Uh-huh."

"Well, you see, there's Mum and Dad. They live here too."

"Oh sure," said Madison. "We'll let them in on the secret, sure we will. They can keep a secret, I imagine?"

"Oh yes," Harry said. He grinned, and without really thinking what he was doing, reached up to his shoulder and stroked the round gray head with his fingertips. "But let's not tell them straightaway. Let's have a bit of fun first. Okay, Madison?"

"Sure, Harry. I'll play it any way you want."

"Thanks, Madison."

"And by the way, George always used to call me 'Mad' for short. You're welcome to do the same."

"Thanks, Mad. You must miss him a lot. I do hope you're going to like it here."

"You bet your life," the parrot said. He nibbled gently at the boy's ear.

"Are you sure?"

"Sure I'm sure," said Harry's Mad.

CHAPTER 4

Sunday mornings followed a regular routine in the Holdsworth house. Breakfast was always boiled eggs. Afterwards, it was Harry's job to clear the table and wash the dishes, while his mother and father went to the living room, she to read her book, he to do the *Sunday Times* crossword. Harry was only allowed to interrupt the quiet of what Mrs. Holdsworth called "my morning off" to make and bring them coffee. Otherwise, he was expected to leave his parents in peace and amuse himself.

On the whole, Harry was fairly good at amusing himself, but there were often times, especially on Sunday mornings, when he thought that to have a friend to talk to, to play with, would be nice.

Now, he was thinking as he finished the dishes, I've got one. He made the mugs of coffee and took them to the living room.

On the sofa, his mother turned the pages of her

book. In his favorite chair, his father frowned at the crossword puzzle, his pencil *tap-tapping* against his teeth. In his cage, Madison sat silent.

"Thank you," said Mrs. Holdsworth. "Have you done the dishes, darling?"

"Yes."

"Thanks," said Mr. Holdsworth. "You any good at anagrams, Harry?"

"No."

Madison gave a loud squawk.

"I hope that bird's not going to make a big fuss all morning," Mr. Holdsworth said. "I won't be able to concentrate on this crossword."

"I'll take him up to my room, shall I, Dad?" said Harry quickly.

"Good idea."

Harry's mother looked worried.

"But he might . . ."

"No he won't," Harry said.

Madison made a small, rude noise.

Struggling not to burst out laughing, Harry hastily opened the cage door and then, with the parrot perched on his shoulder, fled from the room.

For the rest of that morning, and at every possible opportunity during the days that followed—there were plenty, it was the half-term vacation—Harry and Mad talked and talked and talked. In the safety of Harry's bedroom or whenever they were sure they could not be overheard, they jabbered away nineteen to the dozen. Forty years in the company of Professor George Holdsworth had given Madison a great liking for the art of conversation.

Harry learned a lot about baseball and American football and life in Cambridge, Massachusetts, and a little about Madison.

Madison learned a little about cricket and soccer and life in Greenwich, England, and a lot about Harry.

There were so many questions to be asked.

"How old are you, Harry?" was one of the first from Madison.

"Ten."

"Ten, eh? That's great, that's swell!"

"Why?"

"Well, you gotta appreciate that your Great-Uncle George was over fifty years of age when I first chipped my way outa my egg. So I've spent all my grown-up life with an old man. Don't get me wrong, Harry— George was a great guy, I'll never forget him, but he'd slowed up a lot toward the end. It's gonna be a whole heap of fun living with someone your age. Incidentally, why aren't you at school? You on vacation?"

"It's half-term. We get a week's holiday."

Madison rolled his eyes.

"Guess I gotta learn the language," he said. "What kinda school you go to?"

"Primary."

"Primary, huh? I guess that figures. You like it?"

"It's all right."

"Hm. I was lucky, of course. Born with a natural way of learning."

"How?"

"Parrot fashion," said Madison gravely.

"Oh, Mad, you are funny."

"And I had the best possible teacher, an emeritus professor of applied linguistics. Not many parrots could say that."

"Not without a lot of practice," said Harry straight-faced.

"Gee, Harry, you're the wackiest."

And as well as talk, there was play.

"What sort of games d'you like playing, Mad?" Harry asked.

"You mean football and stuff? Guess I ain't built for that, Harry."

"No, no, I mean games that you and I can play together, you know, like cards."

"Now cards," said Madison, "are real tricky. Trouble is, my foot ain't designed for holding a playing card any more than a pencil. Let alone managing a deck of cards, or shuffling, or dealing. No, what I like are board games, you know? Where I can use my beak to pick up the pieces? George and I used to play a lot."

"You mean, like dominoes?"

"Yeah."

"Draughts?"

"Draughts? Never heard tell of that."

Harry fetched a box of draughtsmen and a board from the cupboard where he kept all his toys.

"These."

"Oh, checkers! That's what we call it. Yeah, sure we played checkers."

"I don't suppose you know how to play chess?"

Madison put his head on one side and looked quizzically at Harry.

"Why not, boy?"

Because, Harry was thinking, it's crazy to imagine a bird playing chess, it's just too difficult.

"There's nothing too difficult about the rules of chess, Harry," chuckled Madison. "It's playing the game well that's hard."

"I'm not much good," said Harry quickly.

"Aw, baloney—you'll beat the feathers off of me. C'mon, let's have a game now."

31

A couple of days later, Mrs. Holdsworth came suddenly into the room when Madison had that instant picked up his Queen. Quick as a flash he juggled the piece into his mouth.

"Anyone would think you were playing chess with Madison!" said Harry's mother.

"They would, wouldn't they, Mum?"

"You haven't swallowed the thing, have you, Mad?" said Harry when she had gone. "You'd better check."

"Exactly what I'm gonna do," said Madison, producing the Queen from her hiding place and making his move. "And what's more, Harry boy, I kinda think that that is checkmate."

"I found Harry playing chess against himself today," his mother said later to his father. "He'd even stood that bird at the other side of the board, pretending it was his opponent, I suppose."

"Harry spends his time in a land of make-believe," his father said.

"Well, it's because he's too much on his own."

Madison saw it a little differently.

Typical only child (like me, he thought)—expects everything done for him, thinks washing Sunday breakfast dishes is a week's work, and, from the sound of things, doesn't do a lot at school. But I guess he's a real nice kid at heart. Just needs someone to shake him up a bit (like me, he thought). And I kinda like his screwball sense of humor.

For all of that first week Harry derived enormous enjoyment from the concealment of the parrot's powers of speech. Part of him longed to see the look on his parents' faces when the secret was revealed, but it was such fun fooling them. At the end of each day he would lie in bed, hugging himself with glee at the memory of things that had been said.

"How's your talkative friend, Harry?"

"Oh fine, Dad. Of course, it's strange for him after living in America so long, but he's settling in nicely. He really likes it here."

"I imagine he told you all that himself?"

"Yes, of course."

"Honestly, Harry!"

Or:

"Why don't you try to teach that bird something, Harry? Just a word or two."

"Oh, I don't think there's much I could teach him, Mum."

"Why not? Is he too stupid, d'you think?"

"He's absolutely birdbrained."

And off Harry would go into fits of giggles, falling about clutching his stomach and howling with laughter.

Afterwards, on more than one occasion, Mr. Holdsworth said to his wife, "Sometimes I really do think Harry's mad."

"Oh, if they only knew!" said Harry, after Madison had been with them a week.

"Don't you think it's time they did, Harry boy? A joke's a joke, but I'm getting kinda tired of sitting around acting the dumb cluck in front of your mommy and daddy. What say we blow the gaff?"

Harry thought Mad probably knew best. Come to think of it, Mad probably knew best about most things. He stroked his friend's head.

"Okay," he said. "Tomorrow."

CHAPTER 5

On the following morning, Mr. and Mrs. Holdsworth woke to the sound of music, of a kind.

Dimly there came to their ears "The Battle Hymn of the Republic" played, correctly but very slowly, on the piano, while Harry's voice informed them that John Brown's body lay a-mold'ring in the grave.

"I've never heard Harry play a tune before," said his mother.

"Huh. He plays better than he sings," growled his father, and he pulled the blankets over his head.

In the kitchen, at breakfast time, he said, "Didn't know you were a musician, Harry."

"Didn't you, Dad?"

"Had you practiced that before?" his mother asked.

"Oh no. It's easy if you know how."

Madison, sitting on Harry's shoulder, gave a loud whistle, and Harry began to giggle helplessly. His father looked at him over the top of the Sunday newspaper.

"Harry," he said. "As I've told your mother, sometimes I think you are mad."

Harry's giggles got worse. He began to splutter and snort, and tears ran down his face.

"No, no," he gasped, "that's the one with the feathers!"

"Eat your egg," said his mother, "and don't be so silly."

Madison looked disapprovingly around at the breakfasting family. Not that he had the slightest objection to seeing humans eat, or indeed, generally, to what they ate; much of their food, he knew from experience, was delicious, and he must make it clear to young Harry that plain common parrot seed was only for plain common parrots. But if there was one thing that really bothered him, it was to see them eating boiled eggs. It seemed to him that to do such a thing in front of any bird was in the worst possible taste.

Despite himself, however, he watched their different methods with a shudder.

The woman set her egg in its cup big end up, tapped it carefully with a spoon, and peeled off the shell from its top, leaving a bare white crown like a monk's tonsure.

The man stood his egg narrow end up, and with one brutal sweep of a knife, he beheaded it.

38

The boy did not use an egg cup. He peeled all shell from his egg, laid its defenseless body on his plate, and then, with a fork, he squashed it into a horrid pulp.

"Yuck!" said Madison loudly.

Mr. Holdsworth put down his newspaper.

"That bird actually made a noise," he said, "that sounded almost like a word."

Opposite him, Harry was grinning all over his face.

"Now what's the joke?" said his father.

"Say, 'Good morning,' " Harry said.

"I've already said it, when I first came downstairs."

"No, not to me, Dad. Say 'Good morning' to Madison."

"Don't be so silly, Harry," his mother said. "Let Dad read his paper in peace."

"Oh go on, Dad."

Mr. Holdsworth shook his head resignedly.

"Well, if I must," he said. He looked at the parrot.

"Good morning," he said.

"Good morning," said Madison.

"Well I'm blowed," said Mr. Holdsworth. "When did you learn to say that?"

Madison had opened his bill to say "Oh, about forty years ago" when he saw Harry put his finger to his lips, so he shut it again.

"So you have actually begun to teach him things?" said his mother. "You just kept saying it to him till he repeated it? He said it very clearly, didn't he?"

"Yes."

Mrs. Holdsworth leaned forward. "Good morning, Madison," she said.

Madison bobbed his head at her.

"Good morning, Madison," he replied.

"What a clever old bird you are," she said.

"What a clever old bird you are," said Madison.

"Amazing," said Harry's father. "He's a natural mimic. We might have known that Uncle George wouldn't have bothered with just any old parrot. Isn't it strange though, here's this creature repeating what we say, word for word . . ."

"Pronouncing everything quite correctly," interrupted Harry's mother, "and what's more, if you notice, with a distinct American accent."

". . . which he well might," went on her husband, "considering that, after all, Uncle George must often have played this sort of game with him, and yet—and this is the point, of course—when it comes to the actual meaning of what we are saying, the bird hasn't a clue. Isn't that right, my friend," he said to Madison, "not a clue?"

"Not a clue," said Madison gravely.

"It's a pity they haven't got proper brains like us, isn't it Dad? I mean, he could help you with the *Sunday Times* crossword puzzle."

"Don't be silly, Harry," said his mother. And to her husband, "Off you go and settle down with your precious puzzle. Harry, time for you to do the dishes, please. Put Madison back in his cage first."

"Yes, Mum," Harry said.

In the passage between the kitchen and living room he stopped for a moment, out of earshot of both parents.

"Mad," he said softly.

"Yeah, Harry?"

"Shall we let them in on the secret now?"

"I sure hope so, Harry boy. It's kinda weird, just repeating stuff all the time. Makes me feel like a real dope."

"Okay, Mad," said Harry. "But wait till I've finished the dishes. I don't want to miss this."

He went on into the living room, where his father was already settled, pipe in mouth, pencil poised, and put Madison into his cage.

"I hope that bird's going to keep quiet now," Mr. Holdsworth said.

"Oh he will Dad," said Harry, grinning. "I'm sure."

"Sure," said Madison.

Time passed, and all was Sunday-morning peace and silence. The only small sounds were the occasional scratch of Harry's father's pencil, the noise of a page turning as his mother read a book, and the cracking of seeds in the parrot cage. Harry came in with the mugs of coffee.

At that moment Mr. Holdsworth knocked out his pipe and sighed deeply.

Mrs. Holdsworth closed her book. "Are you stuck?" she said.

"Mm. It's quite a hard one today, really. Listen to this, for instance. I can't think of a single word in the English language that fits: blank S two blanks T blank C blank N blank."

"What's the clue?"

" 'Cat in spite of being a bird.' "

There was a moment's silence, and then, "It's an anagram, Mr. Holdsworth, sir," said Madison in a respectful voice. " 'Psittacine.' Means, 'belonging to the parrot family.' You want me to spell it for you?"

CHAPTER 6

Only a week had passed—just the space between one Sunday and the next—and yet it seemed to the whole family that there had never been a time without Madison. How had they ever managed before, each of them wondered.

As for the dog and the cat, they could hardly remember what life had been like before the coming of the stocky gray stranger with the human voice, or rather, with a variety of human voices, since Madison might, for example, address either one of them in the tones of any of the three Holdsworths. This filled the mind of the dog with awed respect. He never barked now when the doorbell rang, ever since Madison had furiously cursed him for doing so in his master's voice, and he soon learned to obey commands to "Sit!" or "Stay!" even though they came from the parrot cage. Doing as he was told would, he knew, be rewarded by a loud cry of "*What* a good boy!" which set him happily wagging his tail.

The cat, naturally but unwisely, had begun by be-lieving the newcomer to be simply a pigeon-sized bird, and, unlike those in the streets outside, which it stalked but never caught, easy meat.

Observing that the humans soon allowed the parrot out of its cage, the cat waited until they were all out of the way, and then proceeded to creep toward Madison, who was sitting on the arm of the chair with his back turned. Poor cat! How could it have dreamed what lay in store? How could it have known of those dozens of old gangster films (they were George's favorites) that Madison had watched, over the years, on TV? George Raft, James Cagney, Edward G. Robinson—Madison knew them all, but it was Bogart's voice that suddenly fell upon the hunter's astonished ears. A slow voice it was, and sneering; and all the more startling because it was not raised.

"Hold it right there, sweetheart," snarled Madison out of the corner of his beak, and the cat, frozen, held it.

Slowly, deliberately, Madison turned to face the animal, and then he spoke again, even more softly.

"Never do that again, feller," he said. "Y'unnerstand? Now—beat it!"

Its hair rising, its tail fluffed out like a bottle brush, the cat began to slink away, and then suddenly, to its horror, there came from Madison's beak the *tunk-a-tunk-a-tunk-a-tunk* of a Thompson submachine gun and the *zing* and whine of ricocheting bullets.

"I had to do it, see, kid," growled Madison afterwards to Harry. "It was Johnny the Cat, coming to git me. It was him or me, so I let him have it."

Already Harry's parents had come to rely upon Madison in particular ways.

Mr. Holdsworth found him an excellent companion when, arriving home tired from his day's work, he would switch on the television and they would watch the early-evening news together. Then afterwards, while Mrs. Holdsworth prepared supper and Harry did his homework, they would discuss the main points.

Madison had been trained by Professor Holdsworth to take an intelligent interest in the strange, often crazy, ways in which human beings tried to run the world—a world which they considered belonged to them—yet they seemed determined to destroy it and themselves with it. Privately, Madison considered that parrots would have done a much better job of things.

That second weekend the *Sunday Times* crossword

never knew what hit it. Together Madison and Mr. Holdsworth made a perfect team, vying with one another as to who could solve a clue first. Madison was especially strong on anagrams.

And, indeed, his skills were not solely intellectual. He found, rather to his surprise, for he had no previous experience, that he was a great help in the garden. That strong hooked beak was the perfect instrument for digging out weed seedlings, many of which, Madison discovered, were rather tasty. Side by side, man and parrot worked in the long summer evenings. They did not speak, lest the neighbors should hear.

Mrs. Holdsworth had at first been worried over a basic problem. She was not at all pleased to have her furniture and carpets splattered with bird droppings, but, faced with an animal of Madison's intelligence and sophistication, she did not know quite how to approach the subject. She decided to use Harry as a go-between.

Harry was direct.

"Mad," he said, grinning, "Mum says, d'you want to go to the lav?"

Madison looked puzzled.

"The lav?" he said. "Oh I guess she means, do I want to go to the bathroom?"

Harry looked puzzled.

"That's what we say in America. No, as a matter of fact, I don't. But I read you, Harry boy—your mom's worried."

"Yes."

"I'll have a word with her."

He found Harry's mother in the kitchen.

"Mrs. Holdsworth, ma'am," he said.

"Yes, Madison?"

"In the matter of what is sometimes referred to as 'the personal care area . . .' "

Mrs. Holdsworth looked puzzled.

"Have no fears, ma'am, on my account. There is always the garden. And at night my cage undoubtedly merits the title of 'the smallest room.' " Privately, Madison considered that that was all that parrot cages were fit for.

Tactfully, he changed the subject.

"Those cookies sure look good," he said.

"Cookies? Oh you mean my biscuits. Try one."

"Dee-licious," said Madison presently. "A short-bread mixture, I always say, should *not* be over-cooked: it ought always to be this pale golden color."

"You're interested in cooking?" asked Mrs. Holdsworth.

"I surely am, ma'am. It was George's hobby."

"Oh really!" said Harry's mother. "It's mine too. Perhaps you know of some recipes from your part of the world?"

Harry, coming into the kitchen later, found them deep in conversation. "American brownies," Madison was saying. "Delicious squidgy, nutty chocolate bars. We used special unsweetened chocolate but the plain dessert type will do, and you can use walnuts, almonds, Brazil nuts, whatever you like. You break the chocolate into small pieces and melt it with four ounces of butter in the top of a double boiler . . ."

"Hang on, Madison," Mrs. Holdsworth said. "Let me write it all down."

Madison dictated the recipe, even managing to say "and take two eggs" without faltering. Experience had taught him that we all have to make sacrifices now and then for a good cause.

"I didn't know you had a sweet tooth," Mrs. Holdsworth said.

"Tell the truth, I don't have a tooth in my head, ma'am, but yes, I'm very fond of that kind of thing. In fact, I like to eat nearly everything that people like to eat, if you understand me."

"Madison," she said. "I think I'm going to learn a lot from you."

"You haven't eaten much of your seed today, Mad," said Harry that evening.

"No," said Madison, indistinctly, because his mouth was full of delicious squidgy, nutty American brownie.

CHAPTER 7

One immediate benefit to Harry was in the matter of homework. It did not take him long to realize that it was a much pleasanter business with Madison around.

One evening the parrot had flown upstairs to find the boy chewing his pencil and staring at an empty page.

"I'm stuck, Mad," Harry said.

Madison hopped onto Harry's shoulder and peered down at the open book.

"What have we here?" he said.

"English."

"English!" cried Madison in ringing tones. "The flower of languages, the noblest speech of all, the mother tongue that Shakespeare spake!"

"Spake?"

"Spake. Whatta we gotta do?"

"It's parts of speech," Harry said. "You've got to say which word's a noun and all that. In these sentences. Like this one: 'John fell off the wall and broke his left leg.' "

"Tough on John," said Madison, "but not difficult to answer. Here's what you've got: proper noun; verb; preposition; definite article; noun; conjunction; verb; pronoun; adjective; noun. Get it?"

"No," said Harry.

But by the time Madison had explained it and dictated it, with the words all correctly spelled, Harry had learned quite a lot.

"You've got these all right, Harry," his teacher said the next day in a puzzled voice. "Your dad help you?"

"No," said Harry. "A little bird told me."

That the little bird's command of language must be kept secret, the family all agreed. It was easy for Harry and his mother, whose conversations with the parrot took place indoors, but more difficult for Mr. Holdsworth, who often came very close to speaking to his fellow gardener. Once, indeed, he leaned on his spade and said, "How's it going, old chap?" but Madison made no reply.

On the other hand, they all thought that a completely silent parrot might seem odd to anyone visiting the house.

"Just say 'Hello,' " suggested Harry's father. "People expect that."

"I suppose you could say 'Pretty Polly,' " said Harry's mother.

"Begging your pardon, ma'am," said Madison, "but I'd be mighty obliged if you'd excuse me from saying those particular words. The name does not fit, nor the description."

"How about 'Handsome Madison'?" said Harry.

"I'll just stick to 'Hello' if you don't mind," said

Madison. And so, when friends or relatives came, he did.

He had an uncanny knack, however, for sensing whether visitors were welcome. Those who were received one quiet polite "Hello." But tiresome callers now never stayed long. The word of greeting, repeated over and over again, if need be in a piercing scream, sent them rushing from the house.

There were times, of course, when Harry was at school, Mr. Holdsworth at work, and Mrs. Holdsworth out. Then, if anyone came to the door, Madison would growl more horribly than the Hound of the Baskervilles, while the dog itself lay admiringly silent.

If the phone rang, Madison could never resist picking up the receiver. But he gave nothing away, as Mr. Holdsworth discovered one morning when ringing from his office to speak to his wife, who had in fact just gone out. He dialed the number and was surprised to be answered in his own voice.

"Hello," said his own voice. "This is an answering service. If you have a message for the Holdsworths, please state it slowly and clearly, together with your name and number, when you hear the signal. Thank you for calling. State your message *now*."

There followed three sharp sounds, the noise, in fact of a parrot's beak tapping on the mouthpiece.

"Madison?" said Mr. Holdsworth.

There was a pause.

"Aw gee, hello, Mr. Holdsworth, sir," said Madison in his natural tones. "I didn't expect to hear your voice."

"I didn't expect to hear my voice either," said Harry's father. "Have you done this often?"

"Coupla times. When Mrs. Holdsworth's been out, like she is now—buying stuff for tonight's meal."

"And you give her the message when she comes in?"

"Sure. What's yours, Mr. Holdsworth?"

"Tell her I may be late coming home this evening, Madison. I've got a meeting that may go on a bit."

"Gee, that's tough, Mr. Holdsworth. But we'll try to save some for you."

"Save some what?"

"New Orleans shrimp, Maryland ham, and strawberry shortcake," said Madison happily. "Pity about the meeting. Have a nice day."

"I thought you said you'd be late home" said Mrs. Holdsworth that evening, as her husband walked into a kitchen filled with good sights and smells.

"I, um, canceled the meeting."

"Good thing you did. Between us, Madison and I have cooked up a rather special meal."

"I know," said Mr. Holdsworth.

"How d'you know, Dad?" asked Harry.

"A little bird told me."

Harry much enjoyed this, his mother's first attempt at an all-American meal. At the end of it, which was when he couldn't eat another morsel, he watched Madison, who was still peckish.

The parrot now regularly sat at the table, or rather, sat on it, next to Harry. Since he was, through no fault of his own, an untidy eater, Mrs. Holdsworth provided a tin tray for him, on which he squatted. Bits of dropped food could then be collected later and put in the dog's bowl. To eat, he used a dessert spoon, which Harry

loaded for him. Standing on one foot, Madison held the spoon in the other, and dipped his beak in it in quite an elegant manner.

Now he finished the last of the strawberry shortcake and turned to Mrs. Holdsworth.

"That was terrific," he said.

"It certainly was," said Harry's father. "Where did you get all these recipes from?" he asked his wife.

"A little bird told me."

Harry sat thinking. Before Madison's arrival, he had gotten a book on parrots from the library, and one paragraph had worried him.

"Parrots," it said, "have strange likes and dislikes. Some are only fond of men, some respond to women, and others prefer children."

Isn't it nice, he thought now, he gets on so well with Mum and Dad.

"Isn't it nice," he said to Madison at bedtime. "You get on so well with Mum and Dad."

Madison settled himself on his perch in the parrot cage.

"Blood is thicker than water," he said.

"What?"

"You gotta remember I am a Holdsworth," said

Madison with pride. "If not actually by birth, then by
adoption. And birds of a feather flock together. Okay,
George was a naturalized American, but there's a whole
lot about your dad that reminds me of him, even if he
hasn't quite got old George's command of language.
And as for your mom—well, George could cook a bit,
but I guess she's the greatest. That strawberry shortcake!
You sure got the nicest folks, Harry boy."

Harry made no reply to this speech, and it was a
mark of the closeness which their friendship had already
reached that Madison read his thoughts immediately and

correctly. *"But,"* said the parrot firmly, "you and me, Harry—we're buddies."

"Gosh, Mad," said Harry. "I don't know what I'd do without you."

CHAPTER 8

Time passed and Madison settled even more comfortably into the bosom of the family. Happy as he had been all those years in America with Professor Holdsworth, life was now so much fuller, more interesting, fun. In the long summer vacation he had spent almost all his time with Harry, some of it in talk, much of it in playing games.

Sometimes in the evening, after supper, Harry's parents would join them in playing Monopoly.

This was Madison's favorite. True, he needed help in handling the awkward, fluttery paper money; but the shaking of the dice, and the movement, by beak, of his chosen symbol, presented no problems. He did not care for the top hat, car, dog, flat-iron, or boot, but liked always to play with the battleship. And—which is why no doubt he liked the game—he almost always won.

The others might go to Jail, move directly to Jail, not passing Go, not collecting £200, but Madison was seldom behind bars. The Chance and Community Chest cards he drew were usually good ones, but above all he was very particular about the properties he bought.

"Why do you always go for the red set, Madison?" Mrs. Holdsworth said one evening. (As so often, Madison already had hotels up, while the others had only built a modest house or two.)

"Just kinda like it, ma'am,"

"The color, you mean?"

"No. I guess mebbe it's on account of Trafalgar Square."

"What's special about Trafalgar Square?" Harry asked.

"Why, the memory of Lord Nelson, Harry boy, your greatest sailor. George was a great admirer of Lord Nelson, had a whole shelf full of biographies of him. And we parrots have always been fond of seafaring men."

"I find myself very short of cash," said Mr. Holdsworth, landing on the Strand. "You can have my railway stations if you like?"

There was a pleading note in his voice.

"You're going to have to sell 'em, sir," said Madison firmly, "in order to realize the necessary capital. I'd be obliged if you would pay me £1,100."

"£1,100?" said Mr. Holdsworth. "Why, that's highway robbery!"

"Talking of robberies," said Harry's mother, "did you know there have been several break-ins in the neighborhood recently? Daytime ones, I mean?"

"I bet they were all at houses where there's no dog. A dog's the best insurance you can get against burglars. No one would try to rob this house if they heard ours barking."

"Well, that's what worries me a bit. He never seems to bark nowadays. I don't think he'd frighten off any burglar. Oh dear, I've got to go to Jail again."

"Mad would scare them off, wouldn't you, Mad?" said Harry.

"You betcha, Harry boy."

Madison put on his Humphrey Bogart voice.

"Turn around r-e-a-l slow, mister. You move too fast, I'll plug ya, right between the eyes. Just don't tempt me, baby."

"That ought to fix them," Harry said, throwing the dice, and landing, to his dismay, in the middle of Trafalgar Square.

"And that," said Madison, "ought to fix you."

For the first few times that Madison was left on his own in the house after that conversation, the thought of burglars did occur to him, but then he forgot all about it.

A couple of weeks went by. The fall term had started

and Harry was back at school. Mr. Holdsworth was at work, and Mrs. Holdsworth was going out to do some shopping.

"Anything you need before I go, Madison?" she called.

Madison looked up from the *London Daily Mail,* which lay on the kitchen table. He was reading the morning's news.

"You remember we're fresh out of lemons?" he said. "Gonna need juice and grated peel for tonight's transparent pie."

"Yes, I've got them on my list. Anything special you want? For yourself, I mean?"

"Never say no to a Choc Bar," said Madison, who was extremely fond of chocolate ice cream bars.

"All right. I'm off then. I'm taking the dog to give him some exercise. See you soon."

"Sure thing," said Madison. But it wasn't.

A quarter of an hour passed. Everything was very quiet, and in the warm kitchen Madison dozed on the *Daily Mail.*

Suddenly there was a noise. It sounded as though it came from the living room. It was quite a light, tinkling noise, a noise of something breakable breaking.

"Now what's that lamebrained kitty-cat up to?" said

66

Madison, hopping off the kitchen table and making his way down the hall. "Smashed one of Mrs. H's little ornaments, if I ain't mistaken."

But he was mistaken, as he found out when he waddled into the living room.

It was not an ornament that was broken, it was a window. And climbing over the windowsill was not the cat, but a man. He was not a big, ugly roughneck as a burglar ought to be, with a striped jersey and a black mask and a sack marked LOOT. He was small and neat and dressed in a smart suit, and he carried a leather bag.

Madison hid behind the door.

Moving quickly and silently on rubber-soled shoes, the burglar reached out and closed it with a gloved hand.

Madison stood revealed.

Bogey would never have been caught like this, he thought. Me and my big mouth! He opened it.

"Who's a naughty boy, then?" he said in the squawky tones of an ordinary talking parrot.

The burglar did not find it necessary to reply to this question. Instead, he opened the zipper of his bag, and after one quick practiced look about the room, made straight for a heavy old sideboard in the drawers and cabinets of which Mrs. Holdsworth kept all the silver.

Knives, spoons, and forks, creamers and sauceboats, candlesticks, coasters and trays, and one especially

handsome chased-silver rose bowl—Madison had seen
them all when they were brought out for polishing; and
he knew that they were the most valuable things in the
house.

"Stop, thief!" he said loudly.

The burglar turned from examining the hallmark on
the rose bowl.

"Shut up, you stupid bird," he said, "or d'you want
me to shut you up?"

Madison did not find it necessary to reply to this question.

Instead he fluttered up onto the sill of the open window, and took a deep breath.

"HELP! BURGLARS! THIEVES! ROBBERS! FOOTPADS! CUTPURSES! FIRE! MURDER! POLICE! HELP!!!!" shouted Madison at the top of his voice.

Behind him he heard a clatter as the burglar dropped the rose bowl; then he felt hands grasp him. Into the blackness of the leather bag he went, *zip* went the fastener, *bump* went his head against the windowsill as the burglar fled, and Madison, for once in his long life, was reduced to silence.

He was dimly conscious of a car door slamming, of engine noise, of a bumpy stop-start journey in what sounded like heavy traffic. And later the bag was lifted out, and he felt himself carried up (he could hear stairs being climbed) and put down. The zipper was opened.

By now Madison's head had cleared, and after a moment he stuck it out.

He was in a small room, its door shut, its window curtained. The burglar was sitting on the bed looking at him, frowning to himself and rubbing his chin in thought.

"I ought to have knocked you on the head," he said.

Madison was tempted to say "You did," but stayed silent.

"Messed up my morning's work properly, you have. Still, I can easily pop back another day—there's some nice stuff there. And at least you ought to fetch a wad of dough. Parrots are pricey birds, if I'm not mistaken, especially ones that have learned as many words as you seem to have. Which reminds me, don't start any of that yelling again or you'll get it. Not that you can understand a thing I'm saying."

He stood up and walked to a table with a telephone on it. He dialed a number. Madison listened carefully.

"Mr. Lock, please," said the burglar. "Mr. Ware here."

There was a pause.

"Hello? That you, Johnny? Silver speaking—Silver Ware. Wonder if you could do me a favor? I've got a little item for sale, Johnny.

"No, not my usual line, it's a parrot, I just happened to pick up a parrot."

Though he could not distinguish the words, Madison could hear the tone of surprise in the answering voice.

"That's right, a parrot," said Silver. "And he's a good talker, and I thought to myself, old Johnny fences for all the burglars in town, whatever their specialty, he's sure to know some guy in the bird business.

"You do?

"Oh that's great, get him to give me a buzz, will you, Johnny? Thanks a million. I might have some nice stuff for you in the next week or so. Bye now."

Silver Ware put the phone down, wrote (with a silver pencil) a name and address in a notebook, pulled from his vest pocket a silver pocket-watch on a silver chain, and said thoughtfully, "Time for a little drink."

He shot his cuffs to show their silver links, adjusted the silver pin in his tie, and made for the door.

"Won't be long," he said to Madison in passing. "If the phone rings, you can answer it," and he went out of the room chuckling at the thought.

CHAPTER 9

After the door had closed, Madison waited until the footsteps had died away down the stairs, and then came out of the bag.

The window, he found by climbing up the curtains and peering between them, was firmly latched. He examined the fireplace. In it stood an electric fire of imitation logs, and behind this, screening the chimney, was a sheet of plasterboard.

"To keep out the draft that comes down the chimney," thought Madison. "And if drafts can come down, parrots can go up, I guess," and he set to work on the plasterboard with his beak. Before long he had pried one edge of it away, and, peering up, could see to his joy a distant circle of sky above.

At that moment the phone rang.

Backing out of the fireplace, Madison fluttered up onto the table and picked up the receiver.

"Hello," he said in the burglar's voice, "Silver Ware speaking."

"Happywings Home for Birds 'ere," said the caller. "Johnny Lock said to ring. You got a parrot for sale?"

"That's right."

"What kind?"

"African Gray."

"Good talker?"

"Good talker!" said Madison. "Why, this bird knows words you've never even heard of. This bird, though I say it myself, is the handsomest, most intelligent parrot in the world, bar none."

"Have you got 'im handy?"

"Yes," said Madison. "Hang on a minute, I'll put him on the line."

He waited ten seconds, and then in a parrot's rasp he said, "God save the Queen! Rule Britannia! Land of Hope and Glory! You've got a face like a chicken's bum."

"See what I mean?" he said in Silver's voice. "What's he worth to you?"

"I'd 'ave to have a look at 'im first. Where are you?"

I wish I knew, said Madison to himself, and aloud, "No, I'd better bring him over to you. Give me your address."

The conversation finished, Madison was about to make for the fireplace and freedom when it occurred to him that he must not pass up this opportunity to let Harry know he was safe. He picked up the receiver again with one foot and dialed the Holdsworths' number with the hook of his beak.

The line was busy.

Madison glanced at a small (silver) clock that stood on the bedside table. Mr. Ware had already been gone for twenty minutes.

At least, thought Madison, I must repay his hospitality before I take my leave. He dialed again, this time 911.

"Which emergency service do you want?" said the operator.

"Police."

Presently a voice said, "Police. What seems to be the trouble?"

"I've been kidnapped," said Madison.

"I see, sir. Where are you speaking from?"

75

"I don't know."

"You don't know where you are?"

"No."

"What number are you speaking from?"

Madison read it off the dial.

"Well, we can soon trace that. Now—about this kidnapping, sir. Who has kidnapped you?"

"Listen, buddy," said Madison, "and listen good. I'm kinda pushed for time. The guy who snatched me lives here. Trace this number and you'll find him, he's a smalltime hoodlum name of Silver Ware, and I guess you may find some interesting stuff here. And while you're about it, he might lead you to a receiver of stolen property called Johnny Lock. On top of that, if you're interested in valuable missing birds, try the Happywings Home," and he recited the address. "Got all that?"

"Yes, indeed. Thank you, sir. Very public-spirited of you. You have an American accent, sir, I think?"

"Sure do. Though to tell the truth, I'm African."

"I see, sir. You're a black American."

"Well, gray actually."

"Could I have some more details, sir? You're tied up?"

"No, free as a bird."

"You're locked in a room?"

"No, door's not locked."

"Why don't you open it?"

"Can't reach the handle, buster. I ain't tall enough."

There was a pause, and when the policeman spoke again, there was an edge to his voice.

"Now look here, my friend," he said sharply. "You're telling me that you are quite free and unharmed and in a room whose door is not locked, but you're too short to reach the door handle? Suppose you tell me exactly how tall you are."

Madison was by now tired of being questioned, nettled by the policeman's tone, and anxious to go.

"Okay, buddy boy," he said. "You asked for it. I'm nine inches."

At that moment, Madison heard a door close downstairs, and then the sound of footsteps climbing toward him.

"I gotta go," he said.

"Up the flipping chimney, I suppose," said the policeman sarcastically.

"You're dead right, sir," said Madison and hung up.

CHAPTER 10

"Would you like a Choc Bar?" Harry's mother said when he came home from school that afternoon.

"Oh yes please, Mum."

"There's one in the fridge."

Harry got it. "Mad would like a bit," he said. "He loves Choc Bars. Mad! Where are you?"

"Sit down a minute, Harry," his mother said. "Just listen while I tell you what's happened. I went out shopping this morning—I wasn't out long, less than an hour—but when I got home I found we'd had a burglar. One of the living room windowpanes—the one nearest the catch—had been broken from outside, the bits of glass were on the carpet. Someone had smashed it and reached through and opened the window. It was wide open."

"Has he stolen lots of stuff?"

"No. He'd obviously been after the silver—the sideboard cabinets were open and my rose bowl was lying on the floor—but that wasn't what he took."

"What did he take then?"

"Listen to me, Harry. You're going to have to be very grown-up about this. It's Madison who's missing."

"Oh no, Mum," said Harry.

"Yes. Now listen. First of all, I'm sure he won't have been harmed. Whoever took him wouldn't want to hurt him."

"Why would they take him then?"

"Parrots are valuable animals, you know. Priceless, I suppose, in Madison's case, if anyone had known how clever he is, but even a parrot that can only say a few words could be worth between two and three hundred pounds, the police said."

"The police came?"

"Yes. And interviewed the people across the street, who said they'd heard somebody yelling for help. Which must have been Madison."

"You didn't tell them . . . ?"

"Oh no, I said it must have been a passerby who'd seen the break-in."

"Does Dad know?"

"Yes, he should be here soon, he's coming home early, he's putting advertisements in the papers, offering a reward. Try not to worry, darling. I'm sure we'll find your old Mad. Don't you want that Choc Bar?"

"No," said Harry miserably.

The evening was not a happy one. Mr. Holdsworth watched the six o'clock news alone. It was as usual filled with gloomy items, but his mind was on a gloomier one.

Harry's homework was a messy mass of mistakes.

Mrs. Holdsworth, setting the table, automatically put out Madison's tray and spoon before she realized what she was doing.

And though at supper they all made a pretense of enjoying the transparent pie, anyone could have seen through it.

Afterwards, Harry could bear the sight of the empty parrot cage no longer. He said his good-nights and went to bed. Never in his life had he felt so wretched.

"Mad," he said in the darkness, "where are you?"

In point of fact, at that moment Madison was halfway up a very dirty chimney. Like all parrots, he was using his beak as well as his feet to climb, and his mouth was full of soot. But he clambered doggedly upward, taking some pleasure in the angry cries of Silver Ware below, and a last desperate fluttering saw him free.

Black now as the night around him, Madison perched unsteadily on the rim of one of London's millions of chimney stacks.

"Mad," he said in the darkness, "where are you?"

There followed for Madison Holdsworth, bird of letters, cosmopolitan bon viveur, self-assured sophisticated connoisseur of good food and witty conversation, the most unpleasant night by far that he had ever spent since first, as a hideous, naked nestling, he had tottered from the ruins of his egg.

As if to be lost, hungry, and filthy were not hardship enough, the puckish gods of weather now saw fit to play their part in cutting the handsomest, most intelligent parrot in the world, bar none, down to size.

First came the wind, from somewhere like Siberia, threatening every moment to tear him from his uneasy hold. And then, before long, it began to pour with rain that soaked his plumage and mingled with the soot that

clogged it, to tar-and-feather him into a pitch-dark sticky
mess.

Chilled to the bone, black as any crow, and now as
flightless as a penguin, Madison fell helplessly from his
perch, off the chimney stack, down the slippery slope of
the tiled roof, and over the edge to the street below.

Shocked, shaken, and shivering, somehow he managed to crawl from the road into the shelter of a doorway, out of the wind and the rain. There, awaiting the
garbage men, was a stack of garbage composed mainly

of cardboard boxes, and into one of these Madison crept with the last of his strength.

"Guess I'm done for," he murmured feebly. "Good-bye, Harry boy. George, here I come," and his eyes closed and his head dropped upon his breast.

CHAPTER 11

Quite early the next morning the garbage truck came down the street.

At each bin, or in doorways or areas where garbage was stacked, one or another of three garbage collectors would pick up a load and shoot it into the back of the vehicle. Inside, a giant metal grinder rotated endlessly, smashing and squashing to pulp everything that came its way.

Madison came its way, still dead to the world in the cardboard box that promised to be his coffin as it jiggled and shuffled toward destruction. Suddenly one of the garbage men spotted him and shouted a warning, and in the nick of time another pulled him clear.

"I thought I seen something live," shouted the first garbage man.

"It's a bird, innit," said the second. "A dead bird."

"Dead, is it? When I seen it jogging about in that box, I thought it was alive. Ah well, chuck it back in then."

At this point the third garbage man came up.

"Wotcha got there then?" he said.

"It's a bird, innit," said the second. "A dead bird."

"Let's have a look. Funny kind of bird."

"Just an old crow."

"Funny kind of crow, with a beak like that. Show him to old Claude. He knows about animals, old Claude does."

Old Claude was the driver of the truck, a big, bald, gentle man. He looked down from the window of his cab.

"What's hup?" he said.

"It's a bird, innit," said the second garbage collector. "A dead bird."

Claude took the limp body in one large hand. With the other he pulled a bunch of rags from under the dashboard and began carefully to wipe the sticky blackness from the matted feathers.

Gradually, Madison began to appear in his true colors—the gray of the plumage, the bright red tail feathers, the white face—until at last only the beak remained, as ever, black. And gradually, in the warmth of Claude's grasp and under the stimulus of his massaging, a little spark of life began to glimmer faintly once again in Madison's body. It was only a tiny spark, just enough to allow one eye to open for a second, but Claude saw it and began to smile.

Standing in the road below, the three garbage men could not see the transformation taking place, but only the broad grin that spread gradually over Claude's face.

"Well?" they said.

Claude looked down at them.

"This 'ere bird," he said, "is a Hafrican Gray Parrot. Good talkers."

"That one's never going to talk no more," they said.

Carefully Claude tucked Madison inside his jacket.

"Hi 'ope," said Claude, " 'e is."

Afterwards, Madison remembered nothing of that morning. He was unaware of the attention he received in the warmth of Claude's cozy kitchen, of the gentle bathing away of the last of the soot from his plumage, of the blanket-wrapped hot-water bottles that were folded around him, of the heated milk, laced with a drop of brandy, that was tipped down him. He simply slept.

At last, in the evening, a full twenty-four hours since his chimney climb, he opened both eyes to see a face peering down at him. It was a kindly face, Madison instantly decided, and out of it came a kindly voice.

" 'Ello." said the voice. "Hi 'ope you're better?"

Madison considered how best to answer this courteous inquiry without revealing his gifts. He decided upon a simple polite affirmative.

"Yes, thank you," he squawked.

" 'Ungry?" said Claude.

"Yes, thank you," said Madison again.

"Hi 'aven't got any birdseed," said Claude. "Like an apple?"

"Yes, thank you."

By making use of this reply to anything that was offered, Madison had an excellent supper, eating until he could eat no more.

" 'Ad enough?" asked Claude.

"Yes, thank you."

"An egg? 'Ow d'you fancy a boiled egg?"

Madison decided this was the moment to extend his vocabulary.

"No, thank you," he said.

And, indeed, as the days passed and turned into weeks, he found that "Thank you" with or without a "Yes" or a "No" served to answer most of the questions that the big, bald-headed man asked him. Otherwise he kept silent. It was a strain, a severe strain, upon such a natural conversationalist, but he was resolute, set upon three objectives. To regain his health and strength, to fly this nest, and then to find a telephone (Claude didn't have one) and contact Harry. So, much as he would have loved a chat with his kind host, he resisted the temptation.

Once, he was nearly found out.

From behind the evening paper he was reading, Claude had suddenly, quietly, said "Madison?"

Despite himself, Madison half-opened his beak to reply, and then quickly closed it again.

Claude peered over the paper.

"Thought you might be called 'Madison,' " he said.

"No, thank you," said Madison, crossing his toes.

"There's an ad 'ere," said Claude. " ' 'Oldsworth. Lost. Hafrican Gray Parrot, name of Madison. 'Andsome reward,' and then a box number. Hi'm glad it's not you, sure as my name's Claude Clutterbuck."

But when a month had gone by, Madison decided the time had come to leave. He made his decision with great regret. Not only had the man saved his life and nursed him back to fitness, for which he would be eternally grateful, but he had grown fond of him. "Clutterbuck," it occurred to him, might well derive from "Clatterbeak," a thought that he found pleasing.

You're a swell guy, he thought, and I wish there was

some way I could repay you for all your kindness. One thing's sure—I'll make certain you get that 'andsome reward. But home I gotta go.

For some time, while Claude was out driving his garbage truck, Madison had been in secret training. He still had no idea where he was and how far he might be required to fly, so he practiced hard, round and round the kitchen—twenty, fifty, a hundred times a day.

Now he waited for the right weather conditions, listening carefully to the forecasts on Claude's radio for the combination he wanted. And one evening it came. In the London area, said the weatherman, the following day would be unusually mild for the time of year, windless and dry.

All that Madison now needed was that Claude, when he finished his rounds in the late morning, should act as he usually acted.

The back door of his house led directly into the kitchen from a little yard outside where Claude kept a number of animals that he had adopted—old rabbits that children had tired of, and ancient hens who had long forgotten how to lay an egg—and where he stored his coal in a bin. At each homecoming he would fill two battered buckets with coal for the kitchen fire; and once he had opened the back door, the act of coming through it with both hands full meant that it stood open for a few seconds, long enough for escape.

"I sure feel like a dirty heel," muttered Madison, as he waited tensely, listening for Claude's return. "But it's gotta be done."

And done it was, the moment those coal buckets were put down on the kitchen floor. As Claude bent, Madison took off, skimming over the bald head and out through the door. He circled around and then swooped low for two last words.

"Thank you!" shouted Madison, and away he flew, higher and higher over the dingy rooftops.

"Good 'eavens!" said Claude as he stared up at the disappearing figure. "Hi'll eat my 'at!"

CHAPTER 12

For the first couple of weeks after Madison's disappearance, Mr. Holdsworth had made every possible effort to find him. The advertisements he had placed brought no replies, so he telephoned every London pet shop in the Yellow Pages. Quite a number had African Gray parrots for sale, several recently acquired, and these he went to see. He did not tell Harry, preferring to take upon himself the disappointment of saying "Madison?" and getting either a foolish reply or none.

One bird (in the pet shop at Harrods department store) did actually respond to his question sensibly enough to give him momentary hope. It had apparently been brought up in upper-class surroundings by someone who could not sound the letter "r" correctly.

"Madison?" Mr. Holdsworth had said, and without hesitation it had replied.

"Tebbly tebbly sowwy, 'Fwaid not."

It was the kind of affected posh accent that Madison

could put on with ease, and just for a second he wondered.

"Mad? Is it you? Stop fooling about," he said, but the parrot only answered "Dweadfully sowwy," and turned away, leaving him feeling stupid.

But when three weeks had gone by, Harry's father made up his mind on a course of action that was bold, decisive, well-meant.

He would buy a replacement for Madison.

There were a number of reasons for this. First, he thought it very probable that they had seen the last of Madison. Second, he could no longer bear either the fact of Harry's obvious unhappiness or the sight of the empty parrot cage. Third, it was shortly to be Harry's eleventh birthday.

Half a loaf's better than none, he said to himself.

So, when the day came, he simply went back to Harrods and bought the parrot. He did not tell his wife, who would certainly have advised against such a plan. He did not tell Harry, wanting to give him a nice surprise.

Harry was certainly surprised, at breakfast, to receive nothing from his parents but good wishes. Not that he had given all that much thought to a birthday present, he was too busy moping about Madison, but it had occurred to him that his bike was very old, and he half expected a new one.

"You'll have to wait until this evening for your present, Harry," his father said. "I'm picking it up after work."

"He wouldn't even tell me what we're giving you," his mother said, at tea-time, watching Harry, thinking how he had changed since his tenth birthday.

The old pre-Madison Harry would have been in a fever of excitement and impatience by now, showing off, being silly, roaring around the house imagining all sorts of fantastic presents.

But how much more sensible he had grown, trying harder at school, acting more thoughtfully at home. All since Madison had come.

Now he had gone, leaving behind him yet another

Harry, quiet and reserved. She watched him picking listlessly at his birthday cake (from a Madison recipe).

"Isn't it nice, Harry?" she said.

"Yes, thanks."

"Dad'll be home soon."

"Yes."

"Cheer up, darling. Things could be worse."

And before long, they were.

When Mr. Holdsworth arrived home, he put his head around the kitchen door and said, "Stay there a minute, you two. Don't come into the living room till I call."

In a little while he called and they came. On the table was a box. Harry's father raised the lid.

For a moment or so, nothing happened. Then out of the box, in silent slow motion, there rose a round gray head with a sharp, hooked beak. On either side of the head was a bright, considering, straw-colored eye. Mrs. Holdsworth drew in her breath quickly.

"Oh!" she cried. "It's not . . ."

"No," said Harry. "It's not."

"No, I'm afraid it isn't," said Mr. Holdsworth, "but I thought you'd like to have him, Harry. He talks a bit and I'm sure you could teach him lots of words, and anyway, well, half a loaf's better than none, eh?"

"Yes, Dad. Thanks. Thank you both. It's very kind of you."

His mother plunged in hastily.

"He looks awfully like Madison, don't you think?"

"Doesn't he?" said his father heartily. "I mean, all parrots look alike, don't they?"

There was a long uncomfortable silence.

I've done a stupid thing, Mr. Holdsworth thought. But I meant well.

"You'll have to think of a name for it," he said.

I'm sure he meant well, Mrs. Holdsworth thought. But what a stupid thing to do.

"Perhaps it's got one already," she said brightly. She bent forward. "Have you got a name, old boy?"

"Tebbly tebbly sowwy," said the parrot. " 'Fwaid not."

The days passed, and Harry did his best to appear pleased with his birthday present, the last thing in the world he would have chosen.

He realized that his father, with the kindest of intentions, must have spent a great deal of money to try to comfort him for the loss of Mad, and he tried hard not to show how much worse it had actually made things. He looked after his new pet carefully but he could feel nothing for him. He was just a parrot in a cage. Harry could hardly bring himself to speak to the bird, though by now he had a name. Because of the affected way he spoke, like a chinless wonder, someone suggested "Fweddy," and for lack of a better idea, it stuck.

Mr. and Mrs. Holdsworth made attempts to hold conversations with Fweddy, but without much success. True, he would speak in reply to their efforts, but only to say he was "tebbly sowwy," or, occasionally, by way of a change, "fwightfully fwilled." He also had a limited range of comments about the weather which occasionally, by chance, made sense. But he was perfectly capable of saying, on a fine sunny day, that it was "waining cats and dogs" or "fweezing cold"; and once, when the heavens opened, and a downpour drummed against the windowpanes, Fweddy cried cheerfully, "Gwand weather for the time of year! Woasting hot, quite twopical, what?"

He also responded to the ringing of the telephone, saying, "Answer the wetched thing, dahling, I'm too weawy to lift the weceiver."

By chance, one morning about a week after his birthday, Harry was alone in the house. His father was at work, his mother had gone out. It was the half-term holiday, so that there were all sorts of things he could have been doing, but he didn't feel like doing any of them.

If only Mad were here, he thought. We could have a game of something, like Monopoly. What fun we used to have.

Then the telephone rang.

"Answer the wetched thing, dahling," said Fweddy. "I'm too weawy to lift the weceiver."

"Hello," said Harry in the flat, bored tones that by now were customary to him.

"I have a call for Harry Holdsworth," said the operator.

"That's me."

"It's a collect call. From a Mr. Madison Holdsworth. Will you accept the charges?"

CHAPTER 13

Madison flew higher and higher into the quiet sky of a pleasant, sunny, late October morning and surveyed the bit of London that lay below him. He was looking for landmarks.

The Holdsworths lived in Greenwich, quite close to the park. Madison knew, because Harry had told him, all about the park and the observatory and the Queen's House and the bend in the Thames where the *Cutty Sark* lay, and he was nursing a wild hope that he might be able to see some part of all this.

But no, there was no sign of the river, no sign of any park. All he could see was row after row of little houses, with here and there blocks of high-rise apartments towering above them, and the traffic crawling, like flies stuck in the web of narrow streets.

Already the effort of gaining height was beginning to tire him, and so he glided down to the nearest tall building and landed on its roof.

"Mad," said Mad. "Take it easy, feller. Get your breath and use your brains. Examine the pros and cons of the situation. Make a plan. Act on it. On the plus side, you are free, you are returned to health, you are somewhere in London, Harry is somewhere in London. On the minus, you're lost. So waddya do? You contact Harry. So waddya say? Hi, Harry, come and get me, I'm somewhere in London? Big deal, there's only about four hundred square miles of it. No, you gotta fix a meeting place, a rendezvous, some point that you and Harry can both find easily. Okay. Let's find a telephone. Hold on, buster, you just gonna walk into some guy's house and say 'Howdy, stranger, mind if I use your phone?' No, it's gotta be a public telephone. Oh yeah?

You gonna open the door of a phone booth? With your lousy beak, huh? Or you gonna smash one of its windows, like vandals do? Hey, wait a minute, buddy boy— that's it! That's the answer, go find a vandalized public phone booth! Madison Holdsworth, you ain't just a pretty face! Let's go!"

He was not long in discovering his first phone booth—being red made them easy to spot from the air— but when he flew down to it, he found it occupied. And of the next two that he investigated, one was empty but in good repair so that there was no way in for him, and the other had been just too thoroughly vandalized, all its windows broken, the directories ripped up, the coin-box smashed, the instrument torn out. Against one wall was a spray-painted message in large capital letters informing a puzzled Madison that SPURS RULE OK.

But at last, after several more disappointments, his luck turned. He had flown across the green turf of what he knew, from television, was a football stadium, and just beyond it he found what he wanted. Standing beneath a street sign that read WHITE HART LANE was a booth that was both empty and undamaged, except that someone had thoughtfully kicked in one of the lowest panes of glass.

Madison crept in, and fluttered up onto the top of the phone. He picked up the receiver and dialed 100.

"What number do you want?" said the operator.

"I want to make a collect call," said Madison, and he gave the Holdsworths' number and Harry's name.

"And your name, sir?"

"Madison Holdsworth."

"Just one moment, please. Trying to connect you."

Then there were buzzings and clickings and a ringing tone and, at last, Harry's voice!

". . . Will you accept the charges?"

"Yes! Oh yes!" said Harry.

"Go ahead, please, caller."

"Harry?"

"Mad! Mad, is it really you? What's happened? Where have you been? Are you all right?"

"Yeah, I'm just fine. Tell you all about it when we meet. Gee, it's great to hear you, Harry boy."

"Oh, Mad, where are you?"

"In a phone booth."

"Yes, but where? Tell me where. I'll come and fetch you. I'll come right away."

"Somewhere called White Hart Lane."

"Oh gosh, that's North London. Miles from here."

"Then I'll be like the swallows," said Madison. "I'll fly south for the winter. I figure all we gotta do is fix a spot to meet."

"That's a great idea," said Harry.

"Yeah, you ain't got a monopoly on brains, kid. But where?"

Monopoly, thought Harry. Of course! Mad's favorite property. That's the place.

"Trafalgar Square," he said. "Listen, Mad. You're some ways north of the river. Say seven or eight miles as the crow flies."

"The parrot."

"Yes. Listen. Just fly south till you see the Thames, you'll see Trafalgar Square just on your side of the river. You can't miss it, there's the Column and the fountains and the four lions, one at each corner. I'll meet you there. I'll leave a note for Mum, and get the first train I can for Charing Cross. It'll probably take me about an hour. We should get there about the same time."

At this moment, Madison heard the sound of loud tuneless singing. Coming toward the phone booth was a man with a red nose and a bottle in his hand. He was not walking very straight. When he reached the booth, he leaned against it and took a long drink. Then he peered inside.

"Harry," said Madison hastily. "I gotta go. See you," and he put back the receiver and made his exit through the broken pane.

"A parrot," the man said carefully. "Shpeaking on the telephone. Time I shtopped," and he emptied the bottle onto the pavement.

CHAPTER 14

"Harry!" called Mrs. Holdsworth, arriving home. "I'm sorry I'm so late. I'm afraid you've had to wait for your lunch."

There was no answer.

"Harry!" she said again. "Are you there?"

" 'Fwaid not," said a voice. "Tebbly tebbly sowwy."

Propped up on the kitchen table was a note.

Mum. Mad rang. Going into London to fetch him. Back for tea. How about making some American brownies? Love, Harry.

Now try not to worry, she told herself. After all, he's eleven years old and pretty sensible and he's often gone in with me on the train.

She got out the double saucepan.

"Oh dear," she said aloud. "I hope to goodness he'll be all right."

Harry in fact was quite all right, only a bit out of breath. He had run all the way to Maze Hill Station, hoping that there would soon be a train for Charing Cross. There was, and he was on it.

Some uncles and aunts had given him quite a lot of money for his birthday, so that he had plenty and enough to spare for the return fare. He had also put on his jacket (in case it turned very cold), his boots (in case it rained heavily), and was carrying his book bag (to put Mad in, in case you had to buy tickets for parrots).

He was so excited that the journey passed in a flash. In no time at all, it seemed, he was hurrying along the Strand, dodging his way through the crowds of pedestrians. There's only one individual I'm interested in, thought Harry—one smallish, short-legged gray bird!

He entered Trafalgar Square to find it filled with thousands upon thousands of smallish, short-legged gray birds, cooing and strutting and bowing and pecking and squabbling, drinking from the fountains, perching on the lions, covering the pavement in one great slate-colored bustling blanket. For a moment Harry's heart sank. How would he ever find Mad among this multitude?

He sat down on a bench while the pigeons chuckled and gobbled around his feet, and stared unhappily at the

Column, pointing like a colossal finger into the London sky. His gaze was drawn up the mighty pillar, up, up to the pedestal on its top where stood the figure of the little Admiral, cocked hat on head, his one and only hand resting upon the hilt of his sword.

BUT . . . what was that shape that sat upon the epauletted shoulder of Horatio, Viscount Nelson and Duke of Bronte, KCB, Vice-Admiral of the Blue? That was no silly pigeon!!

"MAD! MAD! MAD!"

And everywhere people stopped and stared at this yelling, dancing small boy, who shouted endlessly the word that, it seemed to them, he was. And as they watched, a solitary bird came gliding rather clumsily down from the heights, pitched awkwardly upon the boy's shoulder, and shuffled sideways to nibble, very gently, at the lobe of his ear.

And the boy stopped his shouting and stood still, only raising one hand to stroke with his fingertips that round gray head, while all around them the pigeons settled again, and the noise of their cooing once more filled the Square.

After that everything went like clockwork. They couldn't talk much—there were too many people around, in the crowded streets, on the packed platform, on the journey through Waterloo and the Elephant & Castle on the way to Greenwich and home—but it didn't matter to either of them. They were together again. There would be all the time in the world to talk later.

Harry managed, at a moment when no one seemed to be looking at the strange pair, to mutter his idea for using his book bag, and the parrot popped inside it to avoid the ticket collectors, but otherwise Harry carried his Mad in triumph.

Up the hill from the railway station they went in the gathering dusk, skirted the edge of the park, and turned at last into Unduly Road.

"Nearly there," cried Harry, pointing. "Look, Mad, 137, that's our house!" And then they were at the door and Harry's mother was opening it and hugging him and stroking Madison's feathers and hurrying them into the kitchen and plying them with delicious squidgy, nutty American brownies and endless questions. And they were still all talking away when Harry's father arrived home, astounded to see Madison, who then had to tell the story of his adventures all over again. Until at last Mr. Holdsworth looked at his watch and said "Mad. Nearly time for the six o'clock news." And they all smiled, because one of Madison's tricks was to balance on top of the TV set, swing his tail up and his head down, and press the on-off switch with the hook of his beak.

"Sure thing, Mr. Holdsworth, sir," said Madison. "I'm out of touch with what's been going on. No knowing what may have happened while I've been away," and he got down onto the floor and waddled off along the passage to the living room.

The smile that had been on Harry's face suddenly changed into a look of horror. Not once all day had he thought about Fweddy. Not till that instant, when a combination of what Madison had just said and where he was going filled him with sudden panic. He should have told Mad, explained it all, promised to get rid of the stupid thing right away!

"Mad!" he cried. "Hang on a minute!" and he dashed out of the kitchen.

"What's bugging you, Harry?" asked Madison, turning to face him in the doorway of the living room.

Harry sought desperately for some last-minute means of softening the blow.

"Listen, Mad. I should have told you, it just never crossed my mind, I was so excited at seeing you and hearing all your news, I just never thought to say. It was a present from Dad. I never wanted it. I'm sorry."

"Tebbly tebbly fwightfully dweadfully sowwy," said a voice from the living room.

In the silence that followed, you could have heard a parrot's pin feather drop. Then Madison turned and walked in. He looked up at his cage. Fweddy looked down. Helplessly, Harry looked on. Madison gave a long, low whistle. Fweddy replied with a short, high screech. Harry was tongue-tied.

"Come on, Harry boy. Make with the introductions," said Madison pleasantly.

"Um . . . he's called Fweddy," mumbled Harry. "Fweddy, this is Madison."

"Blistewing hot, what?" said Fweddy.

"He doesn't talk sense," said Harry hastily. "Honestly, Mad, he's an idiotic bird, we'll get rid of him, we'll sell him, right away, tomorrow, we'll take him to a pet shop, Dad won't mind, I'm sure."

His parents came into the room.

"Dad won't mind what?" said his father. "Hey, Mad, you haven't switched the news on."

"Tebbly tebbly sowwy," said Madison in Fweddy's high affected voice. "What a silly pawwot I am," and to the amazement of the Holdsworths, both birds suddenly burst out laughing.

CHAPTER 15

That was all on a Thursday. For some reason that they did not understand, Madison was anxious to know which Thursday in November it was. He seemed satisfied when they told him it was the first one.

When he reached his office on Friday, Mr. Holdsworth rang the police to inquire if anything further had been heard of the thief who had broken into his house, and was told that a character called Silver Ware had indeed been found to be in possession of a quantity of stolen valuables, and had been arrested.

"He might well have been your man, sir," the officer told him. "We've recently had information that led us to a couple of other villains. The same information, strangely enough, that we had some while back, though we disregarded it then as it came from some American joker."

"Joker?"

"Said he'd been kidnapped, was going to escape up a chimney, and, to top it all, was only nine inches tall."

"He must have been Mad," said Mr. Holdsworth solemnly.

He also made a call to the local authority to trace the address of one of their garbage men, a Mr. Claude Clutterbuck; and then he sent him, anonymously, the reward he'd had in mind, of £50.

" 'Andsome hindeed," said Madison in Claude's voice when he heard about this. " 'E'll eat 'is hother 'at."

On Saturday they had a family game of Monopoly. Madison's battleship was in unbeatable form, collecting no less than three good sets (including, of course, the red one), and bankrupting them all.

On Sunday there was the crossword for Mr. Holdsworth and Madison to enjoy.

And on Monday, when the second half of the term began, Harry went back to school with a light heart, looking forward to the evening's homework.

As for Harry's mother, she was happy about the idea of a special meal, a feast in honor of Madison's home-coming, but he said he would rather wait a while.

"When would you like it then?" she asked.

"If it's all the same to you, ma'am," said Madison, "how about the fourth Thursday of November?"

Mrs. Holdsworth was puzzled, but agreed. Maybe it's his birthday, she thought.

All this time, nothing had been decided about Fweddy. Mr. Holdsworth had asked Harry what he wanted to do, and Harry asked Madison, and Madison, surprisingly, had seemed quite happy with things as they were.

"You can't just show Fweddy the door," he said. "The bird's happy here. And it's company for me, night times."

And, indeed, each night they perched side by side in the big parrot cage in the most companionable way. Harry would say good night on his way to bed, and Madison would answer sensibly. Fweddy, on the other hand, would either offer his usual apology or make some silly remark about the weather.

But before long he surprised Harry one evening by not only saying "Good night," but actually adding "Sweet dweams."

"You're teaching that bird a thing or two, aren't you, Mad?" Harry said the next morning at breakfast.

Madison paused, his spoonful of porridge sweetened with golden syrup halfway to his beak. He looked smug.

"You're gonna be surprised one of these days," he said.

"But how do you communicate?" asked Mr.

Holdsworth. "I mean, it's not as though he can understand English like you. He's just picked up the odd sentence."

"It's simple if you think about it. I'm bilingual."

"What's that mean?" said Harry.

"I speak two languages."

"What's the other one then?"

"Parrot."

"So you think Fweddy's going to astonish us, do you, Mad?" asked Mrs. Holdsworth.

"Given time, ma'am, given time."

"How long?" said Harry.

"Coupla weeks, I guess."

A couple of weeks later Mrs. Holdsworth looked at the calendar. It was Tuesday, November 26th, and the 28th had a circle around it to remind her it was the fourth Thursday of the month.

"Mad," she called from the kitchen. "Can you spare a minute?"

"Sure," shouted Madison from the parrot cage. Its door was always open, but Fweddy seldom ventured out, and Madison, the family noticed, seemed quite happy to keep him company for long spells. They would chatter softly together in parrot language.

"About this feast, Mad," said Harry's mother when
he arrived in the kitchen. "You wanted it on the fourth
Thursday. That's the day after tomorrow. We ought to
be thinking about it."

"Aw gee, ma'am," cried Madison. "What with one
thing and another, it went clean out of my head. Mighty
glad you remembered."

"Is it your birthday?"

"No, no, it's Thanksgiving Day."

"Oh. An American national holiday, isn't it?"

"Yeah. To commemorate the feast the Pilgrim Fa-

119

thers had with the Indians, at Plymouth Colony, to celebrate their first harvest on American soil. I just thought it would be kinda nice to celebrate my return home on that particular day."

"It would," said Mrs. Holdsworth. "We will."

So they began to plan the meal, the main part of which would be roast turkey with cranberry sauce.

When Thursday evening came, and Thanksgiving dinner was almost ready, Madison came shuffling into the kitchen.

"We eating in here, ma'am?"

"We always eat in the kitchen, Madison," said Harry's mother. "You know that."

"Sure, sure. It's just that . . . well, I figured Fweddy might like to come along. Seems kinda tough to be left in there while we're all having a good time."

"Of course, Mad. I'll set a place for him."

Madison went back into the living room, where Harry and his father were playing a game.

"Dinner nearly ready?" asked Mr. Holdsworth.

"Yes, sir. Mrs. Holdsworth was kind enough to say Fweddy can come along too."

"D'you hear that, Fweddy?" said Harry. "You're invited to Thanksgiving dinner."

" 'Fwaid I'm not tebbly hungwy," said Fweddy.

"I must say, Mad, you've done wonders with that bird," said Harry's father.

Madison scratched the side of his face.

"You ain't seen nothing yet," he said.

At that moment Mrs. Holdsworth called, "Dinner's ready!"

"Come on, Fweddy," said Harry. "There are lots of lovely things to eat."

"Cawwy me, Hawwy," said Fweddy. "I'm feeling fwagile."

When they were all sitting down, Fweddy on a second tray beside Madison's, Mr. Holdsworth poured a glass of wine for his wife and one for himself and a Coke for Harry.

"Now then," he said to his family, "I ask you to raise your glasses and drink a toast. Let's begin this splendid feast by giving thanks for the safe return of Harry's Mad."

"To Harry's Mad!" they all cried, and then they fell to work with a will. Only Fweddy seemed to have no appetite.

"Fweddy," said Harry's mother. "You're not eating anything."

"Tebbly sowwy."

But for Harry and Mad, who both loved sweet things, the best part of the meal was the Thanksgiving dessert (a favorite of Great-Uncle George's), for which Madison had supplied the recipe, full of figs and raisins and masses of brown sugar.

At last everyone had finished eating and Mrs. Holdsworth was just about to ask for help with the dishes when suddenly Fweddy, who had hardly spoken a word throughout but had simply sat, looking rather uncomfortable, upon the tray, gave a kind of a grunt and stood up.

And there, to the Holdsworths' amazement, was a small, glistening, pearly white, newly laid egg.

The three Holdsworths looked at Freddy.
They looked at the egg.
They looked at Madison.
"Call me Fwedewika," said Fweddy.
"Call me Dad," said Harry's Mad.